The Market at Night

PRAISE FOR *STORYSHARES*

"One of the brightest innovators and game-changers in the education industry."
– Forbes

"Your success in applying research-validated practices to promote literacy serves as a valuable model for other organizations seeking to create evidence-based literacy programs."

- Library of Congress

"We need powerful social and educational innovation, and Storyshares is breaking new ground. The organization addresses critical problems facing our students and teachers. I am excited about the strategies it brings to the collective work of making sure every student has an equal chance in life."
– Teach For America

"Around the world, this is one of the up-and-coming trailblazers changing the landscape of literacy and education."
- International Literacy Association

"It's the perfect idea. There's really nothing like this. I mean wow, this will be a wonderful experience for young people."   - Andrea Davis Pinkney, Executive Director, Scholastic

"Reading for meaning opens opportunities for a lifetime of learning. Providing emerging readers with engaging texts that are designed to offer both challenges and support for each individual will improve their lives for years to come. Storyshares is a wonderful start."
- David Rose, Co-founder of CAST & UDL

The Market at Night

Cat Jenkins

STORYSHARES

Story Share, Inc.
New York. Boston. Philadelphia

Published in the United States by Story Share, Inc.

The characters and events in this book are fictitious. Any similarity to real persons, living or dead, is entirely coincidental.

Storyshares
Story Share, Inc.
24 N. Bryn Mawr Avenue #340
Bryn Mawr, PA 19010-3304
www.storyshares.org

Inspiring reading with a new kind of book.

Interest Level: Middle School
Grade Level Equivalent: 3.8

9798885979122

Book design by Storyshares

Printed in the United States of America

Storyshares Presents

1

Angela squinted, trying to see through the heavy rain.

The acid-green neon sign in the window looked blurry, like it was melting into the Seattle night. Angela looked around. She stepped out from the doorway where she was hiding. She'd chosen that doorway because it was across the street from the shop she was watching.

Pike Place Market was known as "the soul of Seattle." It was open every day except Thanksgiving and Christmas. Most of the vendors, craftspeople, and performers opened their shops from nine in the morning until four in the afternoon. A few restaurants and cafes stayed open later. But now it was nearly three hours past midnight. The Market had been put to bed for the night.

Angela really wanted to know if there was anyone inside the little shop with the green neon eye in the window.

She ran across the wet pavement and pressed herself against the brick wall, next to the shop's door. She looked up at the sign, blinking the rain out of her eyes. The green neon eye flickered. It lit up the words below it.

Curious And Strange Things

The light flickered again, like it knew Angela was there. Maybe it was warning her that even though the eye was neon, it could still see her.

A beaded curtain in the window partly blocked the view of the interior. Angela didn't think there was any movement behind it. All she saw was darkness and a dim, lonely light at the back of the shop. It was hard to tell if there was anyone inside or not.

Angela was tired of guessing.

2

Angela took a deep breath. Gripping the brass doorknob, she twisted it and pushed.

One step and she was inside the shop.

So Mindy wasn't lying, Angela thought. *When everything else is locked up for the night, this place is open. I wonder what else that she told me might be true?*

Angela coughed. The scent of incense was strong in the air.

Pike Place Market spread across nine acres of downtown Seattle overlooking the waterfront. Sea breezes and salt air fresh from the Pacific Ocean were the norm. But in this dark shop, it smelled like sandalwood, sage, and a hint of strawberries.

Her cough didn't bring anyone to see who had come in at such a late hour.

Angela tried calling out. "Hello? Is anyone there? Hello?"

No answer. Not a sound.

Angela shivered. So Mindy was right about that, too. No one was here.

She made her way deeper into the shop, moving toward the faint glow of light coming from the back room.

"Hel— hello?" She hated that her voice shook as she spoke.

When she found where the dim light was coming from, Angela stopped and stared.

It was a wood-paneled room with a bare lightbulb hanging from the ceiling. The bulb didn't give off enough light to reach the dark corners. But it did illuminate one very important feature.

A door.

3

It was a very plain, wooden door. Except for the doorknob. The doorknob was crystal. It sparkled even in the shadowy light.

Angela stepped closer. She reached out one hand and trailed a finger along the door's edge. There were carvings that she hadn't seen at first. Animals, trees, stars, circles, lines, and maybe something like ancient symbols? She couldn't really tell.

Angela took a step backwards. And another. She stared at the door from a safe distance. She tried to remember exactly what Mindy had told her.

Pike Place Market was one of the oldest public markets in the United States. It had been around since 1907. But it wasn't only a place for buying, selling, and entertainment. It also provided housing to some people who lived in Seattle.

Angela's friend, Mindy, lived with her disabled grandmother in an apartment at the Market. The apartments were specially designed for low-income, senior artists. Mindy's Nana Ree used a wheelchair, but that hadn't slowed down her painting. Pike Place Market gave her enough space to paint as well as live.

Living at the Market made Mindy an expert on all things Market-related. Or so she thought. Sometimes that bothered Angela. Angela might not live so close to the Market, but she was born and raised in Seattle. She'd been visiting the Market since she was old enough to take the bus on her own.

So when Mindy told Angela that she'd noticed something weird, Angela thought it was just part of their

I-know-it-better-than-you-do competition about Pike Place Market.

4

"I'm not kidding, Angie," Mindy had said at lunch last Friday. They were in the Washington Middle School cafeteria. "Nana asked me to model for her so she could paint the streetlight shining into her studio window. So I was kinda bored and just staring out at the street. And I saw!"

"Saw what?" Angela wanted details, not some spooky ghost-story fantasy. "Tell me."

Mindy moved closer. She looked around to make sure no one was listening. "It was late. Real late. And some people went into that place with the green eye in the window. They were in there for a long time. So long I almost forgot they'd gone in. But just when Nana said she was done for the day, I saw them come back out of the door."

"Yeah? So?" Angela asked.

"So, they were carrying bags they didn't have when they went in," Mindy said.

Angela sighed. "So they bought some stuff. Big deal."

"But the bags were glowing!" Mindy leaned in even closer. Her voice dropped to a whisper. "And when one of them opened a bag to look inside, there were… sparkles!"

"Sparkles?" Angela asked.

"Like… weird little bits of glitter that floated up out of it. It was totally creepy!" Mindy said.

Angela chewed on her bottom lip for a moment, thinking. "Min, it was dark. You were tired. The light probably played tricks with your eyes. I mean, even your Nana Ree wanted to paint the light from the streetlamps 'cause she saw it made things look different."

"But there's more," Mindy said. "After Nana cleaned up and went to bed, I snuck out and went down to that store."

"And?" Angela's voice had dropped to the same whispery level as Mindy's.

"And the door wasn't locked. I walked right in," Mindy said. "And there was no one and nothing there. Nothing on any shelves. Nothing in the back. Nothing to sell and no one to sell it."

"Maybe it's out of business and the owner moved out," Angela said.

"No, Angie. Just listen!" Mindy took a shaky breath and let it out with a shiver. "There's more. A door in a back room. I could hear stuff going on behind it, but… but…"

"Where did the door lead to?" Angela asked.

"I… I don't know. I didn't open it." Mindy hung her head. She rubbed her thumbnail across a scratch in the lunchroom table. "I chickened out, okay?"

Angela watched her friend for a moment. She wondered if this was a joke. "I don't know what to say,

Mindy. The store's deserted and unlocked. You saw some people wander in by mistake."

Mindy gave a gusty sigh. She sat back in her chair, shoulders slumping. "You just don't get it. There's something weird and kinda scary going on. The Market's different at night."

"Yeah. It's closed," Angela said.

The end-of-lunch bell rang. It was time to get back to class, so that's where they'd left things about the Market. Angela had just thought Mindy was being silly. But that didn't stop her from thinking about everything her friend had said.

5

Pike Place Market was a little bit odd and a little bit magical, at least in Angela's opinion.

The front of it looked normal enough. The Main Arcade was at street level. It was a farmer's market. Meats, cheeses, vegetables, fruit, flowers, and seafood were the main things sold.

One of the most famous shops was the fishmonger's. Whole fish were thrown through the air to men waiting behind a counter. They would catch the fish and wrap them in paper for people to take home for supper. The fish were tossed over customers' heads and through crowds. They flew within inches of people walking by. It made buying seafood a breathless, exciting, acrobatic act. Tourists came from all over the country to see the flying fish of Pike Place Market.

But it was the Lower Arcade where Angela felt magic.

A staircase led below street level, where there was a maze of shops. You never knew what you'd find around any corner. Angela had been awestruck and charmed the first time she went to the lower level of the Market. She'd found beautifully painted kites, jeweled hummingbird feeders, arts and crafts, and fancy teas. There were perfumes, clothing, jewelry, ornaments, and fine wines.

So much to see.

You could spend days searching the Market's corners and never know all its secrets.

As Angela stood in front of the wooden door in the deserted shop, she remembered the good times she'd had in the daytime Market. She understood how Mindy had felt scared, though.

It was dark. She was alone. She could hear something faint coming from the other side of the door. She wasn't sure what it was.

And there was only one way to find out.

6

Angela stepped up to the door and took hold of the sparkling, crystal knob. She turned it and pushed the door open.

She stopped in the doorway, staring. And listening.

She could hear the sounds better now. They were like the delicate, quiet notes that a music box would play. But there was no tune. At least none that Angela could recognize. It was more like wind chimes than a music box. It made Angela want to step through the door.

But what she saw made her pause.

It was nighttime, of course, but there was light in the stairway in front of her. An odd kind of light. It looked like a ghost or an angel had breathed out and covered everything with a soft, pale, sea-green color. It was beautiful.

But curious and strange.

Just like the name of the shop, Angela thought.

The stairway at her feet led downward. Except for the ghostly light, it looked like the stairs that led to the Lower Arcade in the daytime Market. But it was in the wrong place. It shouldn't be inside a tiny shop. It should be across the street in the Main Arcade.

Angela knew the Lower Arcade like the back of her own hand. It was her favorite part of Pike Place Market. And that gave her the courage to see where the stairs would lead.

At the bottom of the stairs everything was familiar and strange at the same time. It made Angela nervous.

She looked at her watch. It had stopped.

That made her even more nervous.

She was about to turn around and run back up the stairs and out to the street. But the shining, sea-green light gathered in swirls and made her want to follow it.

Angela walked over to the first store on the right. She wasn't old enough to buy wine, but during the day she liked looking at the rows and rows of bottles with labels from all over the world.

It should have been the wine shop there, the first store on the right.

But it wasn't.

7

Angela looked up at the sign over the door. Instead of Fine Wine Imports, it said Adam Zimmerman's Rewind Shop.

What in the world is a Rewind Shop? she wondered.

Only one way to find out.

Inside Adam Zimmerman's Rewind Shop, Angela felt the same way as when she'd seen the staircase. Things looked the same, but different.

There were shelves filled with bottles on every wall, only the bottles were smaller than wine bottles and stacked together. And they were all the colors of the rainbow. Some looked very old. Some had things glittering inside them. Angela moved as close as she dared to read some of the labels.

A booming voice startled her.

"Here now! What are you doing here? Lose your way, did you? You don't seem old enough to need a rewind!"

Angela's mouth hung open as she stared at the voice's owner.

He sat behind a counter at the back of the store. Gray hair and a gray beard made Angela think he looked like a professor, or at least someone who was wise in his years. But as she watched, the man's appearance changed.

Dark brown began to thread through his beard and hair. His skin became plumper and smoother. Before she knew what had happened, Angela was looking at a young man in the prime of life. And as soon as she decided the shop owner was young, the process began to reverse!

His hair and beard turned silver-gray. Wrinkles and hollows appeared on his face. In a matter of minutes, the man was old again. When the cycle began to repeat, Angela squeezed her eyes shut.

8

I must be dreaming! Angela thought.

But when she opened her eyes, the man was still there. And still aging and youth-ing by turn.

Angela was ready to run back to the stairs and the street, but the man's jolly laughter stopped her.

She decided that anyone with such a warm laugh couldn't be too scary.

"Hello there! Hi!" he said. "Didn't mean to startle you, young lady. What might you be looking for? What can I get you?" The old-to-young-to-old man laughed again.

Angela couldn't help smiling herself. He looked so happy to have someone in his shop.

"I... I don't know," Angela said. "What is this place?"

"It's Adam Zimmerman's Rewind Shop," the man said. "I'm Adam Zimmerman. This is my shop. Do you need a rewind?"

Angela didn't know what a rewind was.

The old-young-old man tilted his head to one side. "Didn't you see the sign? It says Rewind Shop, clear as can be. I like to say we have every kind of rewind, from A to Z. Get it? A to Z. Like my initials... Adam Zimmerman. That's me."

Angela only grew more lost.

Adam Zimmerman waved one hand like it wasn't worth worrying about. "Well, no matter. Take a look around, young lady. I'm sure you'll find something you can use," he said.

Adam Zimmerman picked up a tattered old book and began reading.

Angela watched him go from old to young to old two more times. Then she decided to do as he'd said and take a look around.

Maybe she would be able to figure out what a Rewind Shop was all about.

9

Angela went to the shelves farthest from the counter where Adam Zimmerman sat.

The rows of tiny bottles were neatly labeled in spidery handwriting. She began to read them.

Just A Second

Couple Of Minutes

Anytime

Yesteryear

Times Of Yore

All The Time In The World

Once Upon A Time

The Wink Of An Eye

Last Time

Yet Again

There were many, many more. Angela was still confused after reading them.

"Find what you need, young lady?"

Mr. Zimmerman's booming voice made Angela jump again. She stopped reading labels and turned to look at the shop's owner. He was still going from old to young to old, over and over.

"I... I'm not sure. What exactly do you sell?" Angela looked at the little bottles again. Some were glowing. Some were dark as night with tiny stars floating inside. "Is it perfume?"

"Perfume! My goodness, no!" Adam Zimmerman's laughter filled the store from wall to wall and spilled out into the rest of the arcade.

"Well... what's in these bottles?" Angela asked.

"Endless possibilities, young lady. And in my opinion, the most valuable, precious substance in the universe," said Adam Zimmerman. "Time! Time, young lady! The bottles hold everything from split-seconds to eternities!"

Angela's eyes widened. She stared at the rows upon rows of glittering bottles. At last she looked back at Mr. Zimmerman.

"But how... how do you use something like that?" A frown line creased Angela's brow. "I don't believe you. You're joking, right?"

Adam Zimmerman looked thoughtful. "There is a time for jokes. There is a time for everything, as you can see. But no. I'm not making a joke. As for how you use my bottles... well, that's entirely up to you, young lady." He leaned forward, giving Angela a stern look. "Now, do you wish to buy something or are you actually daring to waste time in a rewind shop?"

"I... I'm sorry. I didn't mean to. I was just looking." Angela began to back toward the door.

10

Angela was almost out of the shop when she looked at her watch again. She remembered it had stopped a while ago.

"Oh, no," she said to herself. She shook her wrist in hopes the watch would start again.

It was an old watch that had belonged to Angela's grandmother. Angela wore it mostly as jewelry because it was vintage and cool. She used her cell phone when she really needed to know the time.

The watch stubbornly refused to start, no matter how much Angela shook or tapped it. With a sigh, she took her cell phone out of her jeans pocket.

The phone was dead. No power. No light. Just a black, blank screen looking back at Angela. She wondered how much time had passed since she'd begun this adventure.

It had been three o'clock on a very, very early Saturday morning when Angela entered the shop with the neon green eye in the window. There was no school on Saturday, so she wouldn't get in trouble for missing it.

Still, if her parents found out she'd snuck out and wandered the city all on her own, she would be in a world of trouble. She had no idea how long she'd been gone.

Angela was sure her phone had been fully charged when she'd set out earlier that night. *How could it be dead now? And both phone and watch stopping at the same time?* That seemed strange.

But then, everything seemed strange here.

11

Angela suddenly felt like she might have made a big mistake by coming to Pike Place Market at night. A bubble of fear began to work its way up from her stomach to her throat. It was so very late. She was so, so tired.

Angela thought she might cry from the oddness and aloneness of it all.

"See here, young lady." It was Adam Zimmerman breaking in on Angela's thoughts again. Only this time his voice didn't boom and he wasn't laughing. He sounded concerned and his voice was gentle.

"What's the matter? Has something gone wrong?" He stood up behind the counter and swept one arm toward his bottles. "Time can make most troubles go away." His old-young-old face drooped with sadness. "I can't stand to see a young lady in distress. Tell me your story and I'll find the time to help."

Angela decided there was no point in hiding her worries.

She told Adam Zimmerman what Mindy had told her and that she had come to the Market to see if it was true. And, most of all, that she was a little overwhelmed and was going to be in a lot of trouble.

12

Mr. Zimmerman came out from behind his counter. He came closer to Angela and frowned down at her.

"So your problems would be solved if you got yourself home at a reasonable time, young lady? Is that right?" he asked.

Angela nodded. She should have been asleep at home in her bed for hours by now. Her head felt too tired to hold up. It also felt full of all the new things she'd seen in the night Market. It was a very uncomfortable feeling.

Adam Zimmerman didn't seem bothered by her troubles at all. "Well, that's not such a big problem," he said.

Angela's eyebrows rose. "It's impossible! I don't even know how to get home this late. All the buses are on their night runs and I don't have money for a taxi," she groaned. "My mom and dad are going to kill me."

It was Mr. Zimmerman's turn to look surprised. His brows shot up almost out of sight. "Would they? Would they really?"

"What?" Angela asked.

"Kill you?" He shook his head. "My, my, my. That does seem a bit harsh to my way of thinking."

"No! I... I didn't mean... It's just a way of speaking," Angela said. "You must have heard something like that before."

"No, no, can't say I have." Adam Zimmerman stroked his beard as it changed from brown to gray to brown. "But then, I haven't been out there in quite some time. No matter! To the business at hand, I say!"

The Market at Night

13

Mr. Zimmerman moved along the rows of shelves, looking at the fine print on the labels.

"Hmmmm..." he murmured to himself. "Not such a big problem... just needs the right... Ah-*ha!*" He reached to the back of a row of tiny bottles. "Here we go! This will do the trick, young lady."

Looking very pleased with himself, Adam Zimmerman handed Angela a small bottle. She held it in her hand and turned it from side to side. There were rainbows inside. Colors of all shades floated across the liquid in the bottle. Angela read the label: A Stitch In Time.

"What is it?" Angela realized she still didn't quite understand what the bottles held.

"Don't you know the old saying, young lady?" Mr. Zimmerman smiled. "A stitch in time saves nine! And you're only one small girl. So if this can save nine, it can certainly save you. So you see... problem solved!"

Angela didn't see. It seemed rude to say so, though. The Rewind Shop's owner looked so happy.

She looked at the rainbow bottle without much hope. "How much is it?" she asked.

Adam Zimmerman placed a large hand on Angela's shoulder and steered her toward the door. "It's a gift. From me to you. People don't find their way to this part of the Market unless it's the beginning of something. I'm sure you'll be back someday and you can pay me back then, if you like. For now, it's time for you to go home."

They had reached the door of Adam Zimmerman's Rewind Shop.

14

Angela put her dead phone back into her jeans pocket. She held the rainbow bottle up before her eyes. In the ghost-green light of the arcade, it shimmered with rose and violet and blue. She tried to smile at Mr. Zimmerman.

"It's really pretty. Thank you," she said.

Adam Zimmerman's old-young-old face smiled down at Angela. "Just open it up and ask it — politely, mind you — to fix what's wrong. Since your problem is of a timely nature, I'm sure it'll know what to do. Goodnight, young lady! See you again, I'm sure."

Angela watched Mr. Zimmerman disappear back into his Rewind Shop.

Part of her wanted to explore all the rest of this nighttime arcade. It seemed to have as many corners and secrets and marvels as the daytime Lower Arcade of Pike Place Market. Maybe even more.

But Adam Zimmerman was right. It was time to go home.

If only I can! Angela thought.

15

Angela found the staircase and retraced her steps up to the shop with the neon eye in the window. She closed the wooden door with the strange carvings on it.

Outside, it was still raining.

Angela shivered. It was cold. She was wet and hungry and tired. Without much hope, she looked at the little bottle from the Rewind Shop in the light from the streetlamps.

It was still glowing in all the colors of the rainbow.

Well, at least I've got something to show Mindy, she thought. *At least I've got proof that she did see something strange here.*

Angela remembered what Adam Zimmerman had told her. She pulled on the bottle's tiny cork and opened it.

Angela gasped as rainbows puffed out of the bottle and gathered in a cloud around her. In her surprise, she almost forgot to do what Mr. Zimmerman had told her. But at the last minute, she remembered.

"Please, I need to get home before anyone knows that I snuck out!" she said.

The rainbows swirled around Angela. They wrapped her up. Their colors grew brighter and brighter until she had to squeeze her eyes closed because the brightness hurt!

She felt breathless and dizzy and...

When the dizziness passed and Angela could breathe again, she opened her eyes.

She jumped upright and nearly screamed in shock and surprise.

She was in her own home. In her own room. In her own bed.

The house was quiet, just as it should be late at night.

Angela lay back and stared at the ceiling. *Did I dream it? Did it really happen? It couldn't have. It must have been a dream!*

Then she felt something digging into the palm of her hand. She was gripping it so tightly. She brought her hand up and carefully unclenched her fingers.

A bottle. A tiny bottle.

The rainbows were gone. They'd done their work and fixed things. The bottle looked ordinary now.

Angela stared at it for a long time. Finally, she placed it on the nightstand next to her bed. She fell asleep still staring at it. She dreamed of things curious and strange.

When she woke, Angela thought that Pike Place Market really is "the soul of Seattle."

And souls are very complicated things. They have secrets for those who take the time to know them.

Angela loved Pike Place Market. She was sure she'd visit the Market again and again.

At night.

About The Author

As a child with undiagnosed Asperger's syndrome, books were Cat Jenkins's escape, her solace, her best friends. Her mother taught her to read when she was 3. Whenever they moved to a new town, obtaining a library card was one of the first things they'd do. When Cat was in fourth grade, there was only a book mobile to provide reading material. She soon finished everything it had to offer. So, she began writing stories for herself.

As she grew older, she realized how integral books were to her early survival. She wanted to provide the same escape, the same solace, the same friends to others who for one reason or another...not necessarily Asperger's...didn't connect with their peers easily. So when she writes, she sees that lonely, sometimes bullied little girl. And she wants to give her a gift. Reading, books, writing...each has the potential to expand that lonely, little world into someplace fantastic. They might even save a life.

About The Publisher

Story Shares is a nonprofit focused on supporting the millions of teens and adults who struggle with reading by creating a new shelf in the library specifically for them. The ever-growing collection features content that is compelling and culturally relevant for teens and adults, yet still readable at a range of lower reading levels.

Story Shares generates content by engaging deeply with writers, bringing together a community to create this new kind of book. With more intriguing and approachable stories to choose from, the teens and adults who have fallen behind are improving their skills and beginning to discover the joy of reading. For more information, visit storyshares.org.

Easy to Read. Hard to Put Down.

The Market at Night

www.ingramcontent.com/pod-product-compliance
Lightning Source LLC
Chambersburg PA
CBHW071225170626
46809CB00005BA/1937